To Lisa and Mark—my TGBS and TGBB!
I'm so grateful for your support, advice,
and encouragement through the years.
I'm lucky to be your TGLS!
-L.M.

For Allister and Katrin,
who make life pretty awesome.
—M.L.

ISBN 978-1-338-21759-9

Text copyright © 2016 by Laura Murray. Illustrations copyright © 2016 by Mike Lowery.
All rights reserved. Published by Scholastic Inc., 557 Broadway, New York, NY 10012,
by arrangement with G. P. Putnam's Sons, an imprint of Penguin Young Readers Group,
a division of Penguin Random House LLC. SCHOLASTIC and associated logos are trademarks
and/or registered trademarks of Scholastic Inc.

12 11 10 9 8 7 6 5 4 3 2   17 18 19 20 21 22

Printed in the U.S.A.   40

First Scholastic printing, September 2017

Design by Ryan Thomann
Text set in Bokka and Dr. Eric, with a bit of hand-lettering
The illustrations were rendered with pencil, traditional screen printing, and digital color.

"HAVE A WILD DAY!" said a man at the front
as we pulled out our riddles to start on the hunt.

RIDDLE #1

I'm spotted. I'm gentle.
I'm tall as a tree.
A branch full of leaves is
the best snack for me.

I have a new baby,
and she is my calf.

AH-HA!

we all shouted.

"THE ANSWER'S ...

I jumped
on the railing
to get a
good **look**,

and **out** popped her **tongue**
like a curvy blue **hook**.

MONKEY!

I heard a loud **rustle** and turned in **surprise** to a small cheeky **monkey** with curious **eyes**.

He picked at my **buttons**, then tried for my **hat**.

NO WAY, SILLY RASCAL! I CAN'T GIVE YOU **THAT**.

She opened her **POCKET** and pointed **inside.** I tucked myself in and said,

THANKS FOR THE **RIDE!**

WE'LL FOLLOW THE ARROWS THAT SAY **KANGAROO.** THEY'LL LEAD TO MY CLASSMATES AND YOUR MAMA, **TOO!**

TOGETHER WE'LL FIND THEM. I KNOW THAT WE **CAN!** A SMALL KANGAROO AND A *GINGERBREAD MAN!*

We **hopped** down the path to the grassy **savanna** and **spied** a large crowd near the outback **cabana**.

I **popped** from her pocket and jumped to the **ground**.

She sprang to her mom
with a long leaping
bound.

WE FOLLOWED THE RIDDLES AND FOUND YOU ALL HERE!

YOU'RE SUCH A SMART COOKIE! YOU HELPED SAVE THE DAY. OUR JOEY GOT LOST, AND YOU SHOWED HER THE WAY.

I'M SO VERY PROUD OF MY SUPER ZOO CREW! NOW IT'S TIME TO HEAD BACK TO OUR HABITAT, TOO.